Secrets of the Agency

A note from the authors

Hi, it's me, Kendall! I just wanted to say, this is a 2.0. When we first published the book, I rushed through the editing (which was a very bad idea) and realized only when I got a copy of the book that I missed many things. So, now I'm going back and changing them, and got a new (and better) cover! The old book isn't available any more, but don't worry, the only thing I really changed here was some grammar mistakes.

Hope you enjoy!

-Kendall

Chapter one

Kitty sat on some stairs outside of a pair of large doors. She was waiting for her friend, Dog, to invite her inside to the meeting. She had always found his name a bit weird; he *was* a dog, but he was as tall as a human and walked on his hind legs. And somehow his paws worked like hands, but he didn't have any thumbs...Kitty just found it best not to think about it too hard. She saw ten guys enter the room for the meeting, which she was still waiting to be invited into.

She worked for the Agency. It was basically a slightly secret[1] government agency. It didn't really have a name though; it was just called "The Agency." Dog was the boss. And this meeting determined whether or not she and Dog would go to explore an abandoned Agency base. It was from years ago, and apparently has some dangerous objects inside.

"Ms. Kitty, the board will see you now." A guy in a tuxedo with completely black sunglasses said. *Finally,* Kitty thought. *How does he see with those sunglasses on?* She got up and straightened her suit, which she liked to wear because it made her look really cool. At least, she thought it did...Hoped it did. Kitty walked through the absurdly big doors and saw a really long table seating Dog, the ten people that she had seen go in, and three empty seats. All of the people looked exactly the same as the guy that told her she could come in, except one looked old, and one had black hair and a mustache.

Dog sat at the very end, looking fancy with his gold tuxedo on. His face was expressionless, as usual, and his golden-brown fur just looked so soft and fluffy, every time she saw it she just wanted to pet it. But right now, that would be very "improper." So she just took a seat at the opposite end of him.

"*That's* Kitty? Her hair looks weird." She heard someone mumble. Kitty touched her long, white hair and frowned. Dog had told her that she had been in an accident, and it gave her white hair or something. It was when she was about eight years old, and she couldn't remember it very well. Dog gave a look at the guy who had spoken. It was the old guy.

"Let's begin." Dog said. "We have found an abandoned Agency base located inside of the mountain; I think it would be a good idea to check it out."

"You should not go, it's way too dangerous. There are many who would raid the base and kill whoever else they find there." The old guy, Jerry, said.

"I think someone should go, but not you. You're too important to the Agency. Maybe you should just send Agent Kitty." The man with the mustache and black hair suggested.

"Either you're saying that I'm good enough to do it myself, or nobody cares if *I* die." Kitty glared at the man who had spoken. Everybody stared at her. Apparently she wasn't supposed to speak. So she spoke more anyways. "I'm going to say it's the first. The first is a compliment." It wasn't the best comeback, but it still somehow made the guy very insulted. These people were weird.

"I would *never* give a compliment to *you* of all people." He scoffed.

"*Larry*." Dog said threateningly. "Don't be rude to our *top agent*."

"You're just being nice to her because it's your fault her mom's gone." At that, Dog paused. His face showed a very brief hint of what might've been sadness, but it was too hard to tell. Larry smirked.

"This meeting is dismissed. Kitty and I are going." Dog growled. He got up and went out the door. Kitty followed him.

"You can't do that!" Someone protested, but Dog ignored him.

"Am I really the top agent? I mean, we're pretty much the only agents that do anything...but, still." She asked Dog. Dog looked away. "Hey...It's not your fault. He just said that to be mean. He doesn't even know what happened." Dog ignored her and quietly got into a black car with *very* tinted windows. Kitty got in on the other side. "So, what's in this Agency base?" She asked, trying to change the subject.

"Nuclear missiles."

"Wait- actually?!"

"Yep. And all the controls to launch them. We have to get in, get them out, and shut the base off before anyone finds out about it."

"Shut it off? Does the base still have electricity?"

"Yes."

"What if there's someone already inside? Or what if they already stole the missiles?" Instead of answering, Dog just started driving. Kitty looked out the window, staying silent too.

What if someone is still inside there? What if there are multiple people? There are still so many questions Kitty would like to ask, but she was surprised to see that they were already there. This car must be *really* fast. Kitty just took a deep breath and stepped out, walking up to the side of the mountain. "It doesn't look like there are any doors- WHAT?!" A piece of the mountain started moving to reveal a metal hallway with flickering lights.

"Not creepy at all." She muttered and waited for Dog for a minute. When he came beside her, they both walked in. Kitty swore she could hear far away footsteps, but they were so faint that it was hard to tell. Dog went up to some control panels and started doing... some stuff. Kitty got out her axe from its sheath on her side; she always brought along with her, even though never really uses it. And she hopes she never has to. She kept hearing footsteps, and they definitely weren't hers. They were getting closer...

Kitty moved towards the sound and saw the silhouette of a person peeking out from behind the corner of a hallway, though she was covered by shadows. It looked like she was holding something. She slowly stepped in front of Dog protectively; if he was focused on those control panels, he wouldn't be able to defend himself if something happened.

"Hey! Who's there?" She called out.

She heard a loud gunshot and suddenly felt a sharp pain in her side. Dog looked up, alert. Kitty's vision started to get fuzzy and she stumbled, falling over. She heard another gunshot but didn't know where it came from. She felt furry paws on her shoulders and suddenly she was leaning against the wall. Dog was crouched in front of her.

"What happened? Are you okay?" He asked. She thought she could hear a small amount of concern in his voice.

"Yeah, I'm...I'm fine." She glanced down and saw she was bleeding. Kind of badly. "I'm okay, go get the missiles."

"No, we're getting you to the hospital. I already shut off the electricity so nobody can launch the missiles." Kitty hadn't even noticed the lights were off.

"No- I'm fine. Wait- what's going on?" She wasn't leaning against the wall anymore.

"I'm picking you up so we can get you some much-needed medical help."

"No! I told you, I'm fine..." Then everything went black.

Chapter two

Kitty woke up and bright lights were shining in her eyes. Everything was white and she was in a very comfy bed. As she regained consciousness, she realized she was in a small hospital room. Dog walked in.

"What happened? I told you not to bring me to a hospital. And where are we? A hospital!"

Dog sighed. "I didn't really have a choice."

"I probably would've been fine. I'm fine now, aren't I?"

"Because I injected your blood with the Dog Virus[2]. It's deadly to my kind, but it can be very helpful to humans."

"Hm...Will it hurt you if it's in my blood?"

"No. It can't transfer through humans." Dog told her. Kitty noticed he had a syringe of some sort of yellow-ish orange liquid.

"What's that?" She asked.

"Oh, this?" He held up the vial. Kitty nodded. "The Dog Virus, as I just told you, is a virus infecting my species. But... I think I've developed the cure. I didn't mean to bring it in here; I was just walking through the hospital to look to see if anyone of my species has the Dog Virus so that I could test it. Unfortunately, everyone's... either dead or in hiding."

"Oh! I have the Dog Virus in my blood now, right? It's what saved my life?"

"Where are you going with this...?" Dog frowned.

"Well, if the cure gets rid of the Dog Virus, then you'll know if it worked if I-"

"No. No way. Never."

"Why not?" Kitty pouted.

"I made your mom a promise." He said sternly.

"Well..."

"I told her I'd keep you safe."

"Mhm... hey, you know how you say I'm reckless and do really dumb things sometimes?"

"Yeah? What does that have to do with-"

Kitty lunged up and snatched the syringe from him.

"Save your species, Dog!" She injected the syringe into her arm. She half hoped that it did work, because then Dog wouldn't be mad at her.

"KITTY! WHY WOULD YOU-"

She didn't hear the rest of what he said. She felt a funny little tingly feeling and her vision went completely black. Then it faded into a gray. Then everything was a blinding white. She was back in the hospital bed though. Dog stared at her. His face was full of shock, which was an expression she had never seen on him before. Granted, she'd hardly seen any expressions on him before. He stood there like that for a few seconds and his eyes looked wet. He then closed his eyes and his face returned to normal. Kitty was impressed by how quickly Dog could hide his emotions. He walked out of the room. "Wait- come back! It didn't work, I'm still alive!" She yelled, but he didn't hear her. She got up and felt strange, like the air moved right through her. She turned around and saw herself in the hospital bed.

Oh no. It did work. I'm just a ghost, I guess. That's kind of weird. Kitty followed Dog. He said something to the doctors and they went to her room. Dog got out a phone and called the Agency.

"Hey, Larry. Tell Jerry that...Kitty's dead." Dog hung up before Larry could say anything.

"I'm not dead! I- well, I am dead. But I'm a ghost, I think! I'm still here! JUST PLEASE SAY SOMETHING!" Dog looked at Kitty for a second, though she knew he couldn't actually see her. He looked like he was going to say something, but he shook his head. She put her hand on his shoulder, but of course, it passed right through him. Though, Dog's head did whip around. He felt his shoulder, but still kept on walking. *So, maybe he* can *feel my hand!* She put her hand through his shoulder over and over, until he finally turned and said:

"Is someone there?!"

"YES! YES, I'M HERE! I'M A GHOST!" Dog paused for a moment before pulling out something that looked like a walkie-talkie, but much more chunky, with a lot of tiny, blinking lights.

"Is someone there?" He asked again.

"I'm here! Please, just say something!"

"I'm here! Please, just say something!" The walkie-talkie replayed her voice, but it was filled with static.

"Who are you?"

"Kitty! Who *else* do you know that just died?" The ghost-talk-translator, as Kitty is just going to call it, repeated her voice again.

"...Kitty?" Dog said softly.

"YES! Oh, thank goodness."

Dog sighed in relief. "For a minute I thought you were actually dead."

"Well, I mean, I am. But I'm just a ghost."

Dog frowned. "I guess that's good enough."

"Don't tell me you miss me, Cheese!" She called him by the nickname she had given him when she was younger.

"Don't call me that. If you have to call me a nickname, it's 'Chems.'"

"I don't call you that because it's weird. Why do you have so many names, anyway? Dog, Chems, *Cheese.*"

Dog sighed. "Why are you more annoying as a ghost?" Several random people looked their way.

Kitty just laughed. Dog looked as though he would smile. "I need to get back to the Agency." He said, walking away. Kitty kept on following him. She got into his car and he drove away, but Kitty phased through the car and got left behind. *Great.*

Chapter three

A month later

Kitty and Dog stood in a very small, dark room. Empty except for a computer desk, a chair, and some papers.

"So, this is my new office." Dog mumbled. Kitty pushed the papers off the desk. She found that she could still move light objects, even as a ghost, "You don't like it either, huh?" Dog asked in amusement.

"It's too small." Kitty told him. "You're the boss; you should have a big office!"

Dog sat down and pulled up a picture of a small building with an excessive amount of lightning rods attached to it on the computer. "I think I found a way to bring you back."

"How?" Kitty asked, staring at the building.

"First, I need your body back. Second, I need *lots* of aluminum foil."

"I'm scared to ask what you plan to do." After a very strange trip to the graveyard, which made Kitty wonder why she was buried in the first place if Dog still knew she was alive, and a normal trip to the grocery store, Dog drove to the weird building. And thankfully, he found a way that Kitty could sit in the car with him: apparently she just had to focus hard enough. Dog put Kitty's body into the building, which was very weird for her to watch.

"Alright, go in there."

Kitty nodded and went into the building. There were some metal rods coming from the ceiling. Dog put Kitty on a sheet of aluminum foil that was touching the rods. He then went outside and closed the door. Kitty waited for a few minutes before she heard some rain and thunder. *How did Dog time this so perfectly?* She saw a flash of white light before she went unconscious.

She woke up, and the thunderstorm was still going on. So either she was knocked out for a few weeks, or she was only knocked out for a couple minutes. Kitty stood up and realized she was back in her body. She had absolutely no idea what happened or how that worked, but she was just glad it did. She opened the door and saw a very wet Dog standing in front of her. She ran forward and hugged him and he hugged her back. "How are we going to explain this to the Agency? You already told them I'm dead." She asked.

"I don't know. I don't think we can tell them."

"But then how will I go on anymore missions?" Kitty said, pulling away from Dog.

"Well... let's say that you came back somehow."

"I mean, I did come back. But that will be pretty hard to explain."

"I have an idea."

"What?"

"Never mind, I'm just going to tell them."

"Okay,"

"Let's go back to my house."

Kitty and Dog drove back to Dog's house, which was really more like a small military base. It had tall, barbed-wire fences with *lasers* on top. And it had a large iron gate. Most people would find it intimidating, but Kitty found it comforting because she had grown up there. They went inside and to the right were some bunk beds, and on the left were an old couch and a very small kitchen. Somewhere off to the side was a door that leads to Dog's office; he has an office in the Agency and an office here. Kitty sat down on the couch, glad to be able to feel stuff again. Dog went on the phone and came back a few minutes later.

"Well, that phone call with Larry went well." Dog said with sarcasm.

"He hates me," Kitty sighed.

"He told me to keep you dead."

"Doesn't surprise me at all."

Dog paused for a moment.

"When you were a ghost...you didn't happen to...see anybody. Did you? With brown hair maybe?" Dog asked randomly.

"My mom? That comment Larry made over a *month* ago isn't still bothering you, is it? How many times do I have to tell you? It wasn't your fault!" Just then there was a knock on the door. Dog went up to the door and answered it. A guy with brown hair and a smug smile came in. Kitty couldn't believe her eyes. Sure, he was a bit older, but he was still recognizable. "Daniel?!" She jumped up and ran over.

"I am back from Papua New Guinea!" He announced, as if being gone for years and randomly coming back was totally normal.

"*That's* where you were? I thought you just disappeared."

"I can't believe it." Dog murmured.

"Well, some said I was dead, others said I was kidnapped, but I really just went on a long vacation!" He laughed.

"That sounds *just* like you. Leaving on a vacation without saying goodbye." Kitty hugged her older brother.

"Okay, so what'd I miss?"

"Well, where to start? I died, for one."

"I had to bring her back with lightning." Dog nodded in agreement.

"Heh... what now?" Daniel smiled in confusion.

"Yeah..." Kitty gave him an embarrassed look. Dying wasn't really something you'd tell a family member you did.

"Well, at least you're not still dead," he grinned. "What else happened?"

"Uh, some guy named Larry sent me a threatening message. He has a weird mustache and doesn't like me very much."

"Yeah, anyways...I'm going to my office. And I want you-" Dog scowled at Daniel "- to leave. You think you can come into my house after abandoning us?" He said in a calm tone, but Kitty could tell that he was angry.

"Okay, well, first off: I didn't abandon you! I just...left," He admitted.

Dog glared at him once more before going into his office and slamming the door shut.

"...Man what has gotten into him? He was never like this. I mean, emotions? Wow." Daniel frowned.

Kitty refrained from saying *well, you* did *leave us without saying anything for multiple years.*

"Hmm... I'll go talk to him." Daniel opened the door. Dog threw a chair at him.

Daniel quickly moved out of the way. "Hey, bud, are you good? Sorry for leaving unexpectedly. The reason is..." He hesitated.

"Get out of my office." Dog growled, low and threateningly.

"Whoa, whoa! Look, before you eat me alive, I just want to say, there was a... a mission I wanted to tell you about, but I couldn't find you in time." He explained.

"I have bigger problems. Now get out of my office before I throw my desk at you."

Kitty quickly stepped in between them, laughing nervously. "Okay, okay. No need for murder."

"Alright, I guess I'll go to Red Mountain City and defeat the Suspicious People[3] group myself. What a rude donkey..." He muttered.

"What- NO!" Kitty yelped, grabbing Daniel's arm before he could leave. "You can't face *them* alone. Dog might not be, but I'm coming with you."

"Kitty, you can't!" Dog then grabbed Kitty's arm. "You can't go with *Daniel.*"

"Why not? He's my older brother." Kitty thought for a second, before deciding to go the mean route. She was feeling angry. "He can protect me better than you. You let me die on your watch!" She didn't add that it was completely her own fault.

And at that, Dog let go, and gave Kitty a clear look of sadness and guilt, the most emotion Kitty thinks he's ever shown. She went outside with Daniel. "Wow, I don't want to be on your bad side. Did you *see* that look he gave you?"

Kitty looked away, already regretting her decision. She and Daniel took three steps before the door opened again and Dog stepped out.

"I...I'm sorry. I'm coming with you too."

Kitty gave him a hug and they all went into his car and drove to the airport. They went into the plane, and it turns out, Dog had gotten them a five billion dollar private jet in just a few seconds. Kitty took a seat on a *very* comfy chair. Daniel sat opposite of her, while Dog was the pilot.

"I'm surprised he forgave me that quickly. He was *mad*. Also surprised that you came along with me so willingly." Daniel looked out the window for a few minutes. "Wow, isn't this so exciting? We're going to Red Mountain City!" He said, staring out in wonder.

"Weren't you *just* in a plane a little bit ago? Or did you walk from Papua New Guinea?" Kitty asked skeptically.

"I mean, yeah, I was just in a plane, but... *look*! It's an *airplane*!"

Kitty smiled, looking out the window too. Though, she was more awestruck because she'd never been on a plane before. Well, once before. But that was a long time ago. And very brief.

"So," Daniel started, "the Suspicious People are led by a guy named Gordon. He's apparently really mean."

"We're here." Dog said, coming towards them. They all stepped out and Kitty let out a small gasp. The city was beautiful! Nothing like Brookstone Village (Where they lived), which was a very small town. *This* city, though, was a real city. With tall buildings, lots of apartments, and even taller buildings! They took a taxi to one of the hotels, where Dog checked in and got them the most expensive room. It was very large and the walls were white, with gray marble floors. Daniel went in and immediately jumped on to one of the bean bag chairs in front of a really big TV. Though he missed, and fell on the hard floor instead.

"Ow!" He yelped.

Kitty jumped on one too, willing to take the risk. But she landed perfectly on it.

"Lucky." Daniel mumbled.

"Not luck, skill." Kitty smiled. Then the doorbell rang and Daniel ran towards it. There was a package, with his name on it. "Be careful! It could be rigged to explode or something."

"No way! It's a package I sent myself[4]." He opened it up and gasped. "A bomb!"

Chapter four

"A *WHAT?!*" Kitty jumped forward and tried to grab it, but Daniel moved out of the way quickly.

"Hey! Hands off my bomb! Also, let me see... Ah, here it is! My explosive samurai hats!" Daniel said with excitement

"You're even more insane than when we were kids." Kitty rolled her eyes.

"Not insane, just...umm...Also, I got us walkie-talkies rigged with a pound of TNT! How it works, you may ask? Well, let me explain! Basically: you have a password. If you get it wrong five times, it goes boom!" He told her a little too proudly.

"What if you forget the password?"

"I have a password remember-er, of course! Why wouldn't I?"
Kitty sighed.

"Now, I have to go get my clothes washed. There isn't a laundry machine so I have to go to the laundromat." Daniel put one of his hats on and put everything else back in the box.

"I'm coming with you!" Kitty insisted, not wanting to leave her brother alone again.

"Hah! No way. Besides, this is a loner experience. If you come I'll need two motorcycles!"

"I'll rent a bike." Kitty followed him out the door. "Dog, we're going to the laundromat!" Kitty remembered to yell before she left. She followed Daniel's motorcycle on her bike, which she got from a bike-renting thing. She still wasn't sure how he got the motorcycle, though. He kept doing sharp turns and he was going really fast. It seemed like he was trying to lose her. Eventually, he succeeded; Kitty had completely lost sight of him. Suddenly someone tackled her, throwing her onto the concrete. He had a black mask on and then he punched her in the face, knocking her out before she could fight back.

At the laundromat...

"Ah, what a beautiful place..." Daniel said. "Put in my clothes and- what is that!? A tilted over locker? That bothers me very much... I'm going to fix it." He mumbled to himself while walking over there. "OH MY GOSH! A SECRET TRAP DOOR!" Before he could open it he got a call from Kitty[5].

"This is the leader of the Suspicious People-" A guy with a British accent said.

"What? Where's Kitty?!"

"Please, don't interrupt me. I kidnapped her and trapped her in a building rigged to explode at three today. Here are the coordinates:" The leader of the Suspicious People then told Daniel a bunch of numbers. He forgot them a few seconds after. He hoped they weren't important. "Good luck finding your friend!" *Uh-oh. How am I going to tell Dog about this?*

At the hotel...

Dog was sitting at his computer desk when Daniel burst in, nearly breaking the door. "Be careful! That door alone costs more that's in your wallet right now. Which isn't saying much...But it's expensive!"

"What I have to tell you is more important than a door! Some guy kidnapped Kitty. He's going to blow her up at three!"

"What-?! Who?"

"The leader of the Suspicious People!"

"Where?!"

"I don't know. He told me a bunch of numbers but I forgot them."

"THOSE WERE THE COORDINATES!" Dog shook his head and turned back to the computer.

"Now's not the time for computer games! We have to go and save her!"

"I'm looking up where the Suspicious People have trapped people before. It looks like...the gas station. What time is it?"

"How am I supposed to know? You're the one with the computer!"

Dog rolled his eyes. "It's two forty-five. We have to get going." He rented a Lamborghini and drove to the gas station. They both got out of the car and ran to the door, but it was locked.

"Hello! I'm Gordon. Nice to meet you." Someone said from behind them. Dog whipped around and a tall man with blonde hair, a fancy suit, and a British accent stood in front of him. "Your friend is in there. It's almost three. You should probably step away a bit, unless you want to die too."

"What- why are you acting nice?" Daniel asked.

"Well I don't want to be impolite."

"You're about to *kill* our friend. I would call that impolite." Dog turned around and started trying to kick the door down.

"Stop! You're going to ruin the door. The gas station owner wouldn't appreciate that." Gordon frowned.

"YOU'RE LITERALLY ABOUT TO BLOW IT UP!"

"Well, you don't have to point it out so rudely." Gordon scoffed.

Dog gave him an annoyed sigh. "If we can't break the door down, how do we get in and save her?"

"Well, you're not supposed to. But I'll let her go, IF you surrender the entire Agency to me."

"I can't do that! What if I just give you one of the board members? I'm sure you'll love hanging out with Larry! Or even Jerry. Heck, I'll even give you Harry!"

"I'm afraid you're missing the point here. I need the *entire* Agency. All their information, employees, bases, and weapons. Oh, it's two fifty-five now."

"I *can't* give you the entire Agency." He told Gordon.

Gordon shrugged. "I guess you'll lose this agent then."

"Come on, Dog! You *have* to give him the Agency!" Daniel pleaded.

"I *can't*!"

"You *can't* let Kitty explode either!"

"Funny words coming from a guy that left her without a single word of warning."

"Now it's two fifty-seven." Gordon mentioned unhelpfully. Suddenly the window of the gas station shattered. It looked like Kitty had just jumped through it.

"Ow. Should've used the chair." She mumbled. Gordon looked up in surprise.

"No! The window! It was so pretty..."

"What's pretty is you in jail! Oh, wait, that sounds weird..." Kitty jumped at Gordon and he swiftly dodged.

"Quite rude." And then the gas station exploded.

Chapter five

Kitty was pushed back by the explosion and slammed against a gas pump. Everything was in flames. She couldn't see anything or anybody. "DOG?! DANIEL?!" She cried out, but she doubted anyone could hear her over the roar of the fire.

From behind her, there was a second explosion. Then a third. Then a fourth. She really hoped that Dog and Daniel weren't anywhere near the gas pumps. Because that *really* hurt. Good thing her suit was fireproof. Couldn't say the same about her hair, though. She put her hands up to her head and put the flame out, and tried to find a path through the fire. Kitty was in bad enough condition already, so she just walked right through it. She had tiny shards of glass embedded in her skin, pretty bad burns on both her hands, and she was inhaling nothing but smoke.

She eventually made it out onto the grass. But the grass was on fire too, so that didn't do much good. She started hearing sirens coming, and assumed they were fire trucks. *Took them long enough.* The sirens were really loud now, and she heard what she hoped was a hose putting out the fire. Kitty just collapsed onto the grass, which would've been comfy, but the grass was still burning... oh well, beggars can't be choosers. She finally passed out, which she was very glad for. She was pretty tired.

After what felt like seconds, but was probably hours, she finally woke up. She was in a hospital with bandages literally everywhere. Kitty turned her head, which hurt a bit, and saw Dog and Daniel sitting on chairs next to her. The tips of Dog's fur were singed and Daniel had slight burns on his clothes and face. It looked like Kitty had gotten the worst of it.

"You're awake!" Daniel smiled at her.

"Did you catch Gordon?" She asked.

"Well, *we* didn't, but the police did."

"We arrested him, so now we get to go home." Dog said, getting up. "Come on."

"Um, I don't think I can stand..." Kitty gestured to the bandages on her legs. Dog sighed. He left the room and came back a few minutes later with a wheelchair. Daniel helped her on. "Ah, this is nice. Relaxing while you two push me around." She leaned back. She probably *could* walk, but wheelchairs are fun. Daniel and Dog both rolled their eyes at the same time. Kitty laughed. They left the hospital and boarded another private jet.

"Back to Brookstone village!" Daniel said cheerfully. After a pretty short plane ride, they were back in Brookstone. They went back to Dog's house, but something was off. Larry was standing in front of it, putting up a sign that said "Property of the Agency" Dog ran forward.

"What are you doing?!" He growled. Larry smiled slyly.

"This house belongs to the boss of the Agency. And after you were gone for so long, without telling us..."

"I was gone for like, two hours!"

"Mr. Dog. I'm afraid the board has decided to fire you."

"What?! They can't do that!" Kitty glared at Larry.

"Of course we can. Me, Jerry, Harry, Garry, Barry, Perry, Terry, Karry, Darry, Merry, Eugene, and Pablo all decided."

"Where am I going to live, then?" Dog frowned.

"Not my problem. But if *she's*" Larry pointed at Kitty "going with you, I suggest somewhere far, *far* away."

"Hey! If you're going to be rude to my sister, I'm going to put *you* somewhere far, far away!" Daniel took a threatening step forward.

"Um, who are you again?"

"I'm Daniel, I have exploding hats." He took off his hat slowly.

Larry laughed. "You expect me to be scared of you? I have exploding bananas!" Larry then took a banana out of his pocket.

"Everyone, get away! This man has a banana!" Daniel yelled.

"Daniel, he's just making fun of you." Kitty told him. Larry got into his very expensive looking golden McLaren and drove away.

"That was mine." Dog growled.

"Well...you still have all your money, right?" Kitty asked him. "We can buy another house...and whatever that car was..."

"No." Dog clenched his fists. "All my money was supplied by the Agency; they pay for everything I buy, so I don't have any money for myself."

"Oof, well I have twelve dollars I can give you." Daniel offered.

"The Agency paid me twenty dollars a month and I've been working there for three years. So I can give you... seven hundred twenty dollars." Kitty said, getting out her wallet. She only then realized that keeping all her money in her wallet probably wasn't the smartest idea.

"Thanks..." Dog took the money and got out his phone. "There's a small cabin we can get for exactly that much, but it doesn't have any electricity, water, or AC."

"Well, at least it's a house."

Dog purchased the house and they all walked there. Well, Dog and Daniel walked there. Kitty was still in her wheelchair. After what felt like six hours of walking, but probably wasn't even half that much, they were there. It was a pretty small cabin, but it was by a lake. Which was bad because Kitty had hydrophobia. But it was fine, as long as they didn't go swimming. They went inside the cabin and there were two bunk beds, a small dining table which seated four people, and a very small kitchen with a wood-burning stove and an ice bucket, which was apparently the fridge. Then there was the bathroom. It had a normal toilet, which surprised Kitty until she realized there was no water in it. That would be interesting. And for the sink, there was just a bucket hanging on the wall. Over to the side, there was a bathtub that you were supposed to hand-fill with water and a bucket. Why did everything include a bucket? She went back to the main room, where Daniel had already fallen asleep.

There was a knock on the door and Dog went to open it. It was Larry. Dog slammed the door in his face.

"Hey! Let me in!" Larry yelled. Dog reluctantly opened the door. "Hmph. So, you know that Agency base you explored a little bit ago?

Well, someone got in and they're launching the nuclear missiles in five minutes."

"What?! I shut off the electricity!"

"You obviously forgot about the backup reserves. Anyways, Jerry sent me to come get you. He gave you the keys to your own private bunker." Larry handed Dog some keys then left without telling Dog where the bunker was. But Dog seemed to know. Larry had, thankfully, left them a car. Kitty woke Daniel up and they all drove to the bunker. It was actually quite big. There was a large kitchen with a walk-in fridge, a really nice bathroom, three bedrooms, a pretty big indoor garden, along with a bunch of storage.

"So, that was very random." Kitty said. "And weird. But at least we have a better house now."

"It's not better! It's horrible! THERE'S NO INTERNET!" Daniel cried.

"Oh come on, you can live without the internet for a little while."

"No I can't!" Daniel ran towards the door and tried to open it.

"DANIEL- THERE ARE *NUCLEAR MISSILES* GOING OFF!"

"It's locked! DOG! UNLOCK THE DOOR!"

"What? I didn't lock it." Dog went up to the door and tried to unlock it, but the keys wouldn't work. "That's weird..." Dog suddenly turned around. "Do you guys hear that?"

"Hear what?" Kitty asked.

"There's a...a beeping noise. IT'S A BOMB! GET DOWN!" Everyone got down on the floor and waited for a few seconds.

"Relax, it wasn't a bomb. Nothing has explo-" Daniel was cut off by a loud explosion. Not one, but many. In all of the bedrooms, one in the kitchen, and one right where they were. Luckily, it was far enough away so it didn't really hurt them, *and* it somehow blew the doors open. Which was weird, because this was a bunker...Obviously it wasn't made to be one though.

"LARRY SENT US TO A DEATH TRAP!" Daniel yelled. "There's no internet!"

Dog growled. "Let's go home. If this was a trap, then there's a good chance that there aren't any missiles. The car's gone; I guess Larry took it. Kitty, you're walking this time." Kitty shrugged and got up off her wheelchair, and surprisingly, her legs didn't hurt at all. They all walked back and Daniel said some pretty mean things about Larry. Some of which including "Weird caterpillar" and "Black licorice donkey". They got back to the cabin and Daniel complained that he was hungry, but there wasn't any food.

"I'll go get some, I guess." Kitty sighed. She walked to the grocery store and bought some bread; the only thing she could afford with Daniel's money. She was walking back when she saw a man in all-black clothes with a hood and a black Japanese fox mask. He was staring right at her. Somehow she got knocked unconscious.

Chapter six

She woke up and she was in an office with the man in the mask. "Who are you?" She asked. He shook his head.

"I'm the one asking the questions. You can call me the Master, and I-"

"Yeah, there's no way I'm calling you that."

"Stop! Don't interrupt me! I have taken over Brookstone Village. You've been knocked out for days and I just need you to tell me one thing. If you refuse to answer, then..." He pulled out a sword as big as him, if not bigger, with glowing red edges. "Now tell me...WHERE IS AGENT DOG?!" He yelled.

"I don't know! He- uh, he's on a mission- in...in Italy. Yeah."

The Master sighed. "I know he's not, so just tell me where he is."

"Well I'm not going to, so you should just let me go."

"Oh! Good idea, I let you go, you go to Dog, and I will follow."

Kitty frowned. The Master then knocked her out.

Kitty woke up in a small bedroom, all tied up. "Hey! You're up!" A familiar voice said.

"Daniel?!" She asked in horror, turning around to see her brother, also tied up. "Why- how are you here?"

"Oh! Funny story. After you didn't come back, I went to get some tacos, and then went to look for you. And this weird guy shoved me in a car, so here I am!"

Kitty sighed in annoyance. "Where's Dog?"

"That's what I'd like to know." The Master said, coming in. He pointed the big sword at Daniel.

"DON'T YOU *DARE* HURT HIM!" Kitty yelled. The Master just laughed.

"Where'd you get that? I want one!" Daniel stared at the sword in delight.

"*Daniel*!"

The Master handed Kitty a phone. "You better let him know where you are…If he came to me that'd be a lot simpler than me tracking him down."

Kitty called Dog. "Hey, Dog,"

"Kitty!" He answered. "Where are you and Daniel?"

"It's okay. We're fine. Don't worry; we'll come back in a few… days." She told him before hanging up. The Master stared at her for a moment, and then turned to Daniel.

"Just *tell me* where Agent Dog is!"

"Oh. I don't know. Anyways, these ropes are really bad. I already got out of them." Daniel smiled mischievously, holding up his hands, which were rope-free. The Master growled, lunging the sword at him.

"Hey!" Daniel jumped out of the way.

"Daniel! Run!" Kitty told him. Daniel raced out the door and The Master followed him. Kitty broke the ropes. *Wow, these* are *really bad ropes.* She thought as she raced after them. The Master and Daniel stood in the living room, facing each other. Kitty jumped forward and punched the Master. He whipped around before she made contact and he hit her with the sword, which *really* hurt. Kitty felt the blade dig into her side and warm liquid seeping into her shirt. She fell to the ground, not unconscious, but somehow paralyzed, like the sword had some sort of immobilizing poison.

"KITTY! NO!" Daniel yelled. Her vision had become too blurry to make out anything other than fuzzy blobs. "Kitty! Are you okay? Talk to me!"

"I'm fine." She tried to say, but her lips wouldn't move.

"I won't ask a third time…WHERE. IS. AGENT. DOG?!" The Master yelled.

"You- you just…" Kitty heard a tremble in his voice that almost made *her* cry.

"I see you are unwilling to answer my question. Very well, I'll give you some time to make the right decision." Kitty assumed The Master left, since she didn't hear him anymore.

Back with Dog...

Dog sat in the cabin, waiting for Daniel and Kitty. Kitty had called him earlier, saying she was okay and would be back home in a few days, but he wasn't quite sure. After waiting for a few more hours, he decided to track the signal of her call with his phone: the one thing Larry had left him with. The signal showed that the call was made not far away from here, so he decided to steal a motorcycle and go, leaving a note where the motorcycle had been saying that the Agency would pay for it. He arrived at a small house and entered because the front door wasn't locked.

"D-Dog? Is that you?" It took Dog a few seconds to realized that it was Daniel who had spoked. Dog had never heard his voice sound so small.

"Daniel? Where's Kit-" He saw Daniel crouching down by Kitty, who was unconscious on the floor. At least, he hoped she was unconscious. She was bleeding all along her body, and Daniel was making a useless attempt to wipe his tears next to her. "KITTY!" He cried out, "What happened?! Is she okay?!"

"No...No, she's not okay! This never would've happened if you hadn't...uh, if you hadn't done something! I don't know what you did, but it's your fault."

"*My* fault?! You're the one who went to rescue her. This doesn't look like she was rescued to me."

"Well...I tried. But you know how she is, so...She rescued me instead. *I'd* be dead if it wasn't for her."

"I'd rather you than her." Dog growled.

"WELL IF I HAD A CHOICE THEN THAT'S THE WAY IT WOULD'VE BEEN!" Daniel yelled.

"My gosh, stop fighting...OH! HEY! I can move again! Finally!" Kitty said, sitting up and wincing as she held her hand to her side.

"Wait- what?" Daniel stared in confusion at his sister.

"Kitty, what the heck were you thinking?!" Dog frowned at her, apparently trying to hide the fact that he was probably on the verge of tears.

"Don't tell me you guys were worried about me!" Kitty smiled, trying to lighten the mood, but her smile slowly faded as she looked at Daniel's somber expression while he looked at her injury.

"Shut up, I wasn't worried." He looked away.

"Well... I should probably see a doctor."

Dog nodded. "It's a wonder you haven't died from blood loss, if not the injury itself, yet."

Daniel's expression brightened as her turned back to his old self. "Don't worry, I have... a med-kit! When I went to the University of Brookstone, I took a medical major." He smiled.

"Wait...you went to a university?" Dog looked at him. Daniel ignored the question and just started to clean the cut.

"Um... shouldn't I take my shirt off so you can treat it better?"

"NO-" Daniel said instantly.

"But then you won't be able to clean the whole wound..."

Daniel ignored her. "Sheesh, that sword did some damage." He muttered. "Now, I just got to take this with a cotton ball." He said, very focused. He opened the rest of the medical bag. "Dog, give me a cotton ball. This is a pretty bad cut..." Dog handed him what he requested, leaving Kitty to question why Dog just happened to have a cotton ball.

"Are you sure you know what you're doing?" He asked skeptically.

"Yep! Positive. Now I need some cleaning alcohol... and another cotton ball." Dog, again gave him the stuff he needed. "Sheesh, there is a lot of dirt in the cut..." He proceeded to scrub the cut really hard, which probably hurt a lot.

"Ow! Be gentler." Kitty glared at him, confirming that it did indeed hurt.

"If I'm gentle, I won't effectively get out all the stuff that can cause an infection, which would really hurt!" Daniel explained.

"Okay, but, I don't think this is how you clean it!" Daniel just ignored her, continuing to scrub it.

After a long time of scrubbing the cut, Daniel finally bandaged it. "And that should do it! Anyways, you guys should probably get out of here in case that 'The Master' guy comes back. *I'm* going to Hawaii!"

"What? After *all* that you can't just leave us again!" Kitty told him.

"Sorry, but I've already bought the plane tickets and booked a hotel." Daniel smiled apologetically as he walked out. Kitty frowned.

"It's okay; we've been alright without him for the past eighteen years." Dog said, helping Kitty up. "That cabin we got was actually a rental, and we don't have enough money to keep it. So we have to find somewhere else to live."

"*Seven hundred twenty dollars* a month for *that* thing?"

"Yes...But I *did* find an apartment in Red Mountain City that's free for members of the Agency. Apparently, they were so glad we took care of Gordon that they're not charging us anything. And the plane rides are free too."

"That's suspiciously lucky!" Kitty smiled. They walked to the airport, and Dog offered to carry Kitty, but she said she was fine. And she wasn't lying... it was weird, but she actually did feel completely fine. They got on the plane, which didn't have anyone else on it. Again, *suspiciously* lucky. As soon as they sat down, Dog gave her an angry look.

"Care to apologize?"

"Uh, apologize? For what?"

"For lying to me." He growled.

"Lying? When did I-"

"You said you were okay! But you weren't!"

"I was- *AM*- I *am* okay."

"Key word: 'was.'"

"I was okay. And I am okay." Kitty glared at him.

"Then explain the bandages? Explain why I found you *nearly dead*."

"Hey- I'm alive!"

The plane landed before Dog had a chance to respond, but she could tell he was still angry. They both walked to the apartments and got their free room.

"I'm going to go grocery shopping." Kitty said, about to walk out. But Dog grabbed her arm.

"Correction, *I'm* going to go grocery shopping. *You're* staying here. Where it's safe."

"That's not fair! Are you...are you *grounding* me?"-Dog nodded-"You can't do that! You're not my dad."

"I might not be, but I'm your legal guardian."

"Wait- what?! When did that happen?"

"After... after your mom died, I signed up to be your legal guardian." Dog paused, frowning for a moment. "It was the least I could do."

"So you sign up to be my legal guardian, and then you just leave me with my brothers for the rest of my life? The only reason you started actually taking care of me was when one of them died and I almost did too[6]." Kitty stomped off to her room. Sure, she was acting like a teenager, but... uh... Kitty heard Dog leave and contemplated going to the grocery store anyways just to prove her point, but that was when she heard a window shatter. She grabbed her axe and slowly crept towards the sound. The window was broken, but there wasn't anything else there except the glass shards on the floor.

"Ah, Agent Kitty. I've been looking for you." A familiar voice said from behind her. She turned around and glared at Larry, who was staring at the glass shards very intently, as if he was going to eat one or something.

"You're literally a weirdo. You know that, right? What, have you been stalking me or something?"

"What?! No!" He looked at her and frowned. "Maybe. Anyways, I need to kidnap you now."

"Wait- what-" Larry knocked her out before she could finish.

29

Chapter seven

Before Dog left the apartments, he sighed; he felt bad about just leaving. He didn't want Kitty to be mad at him, so he decided to go back up to his apartment. He went in, but the window was broken. *She didn't run away... did she?!* Dog looked around the apartment for her, before realizing that the glass shards were on the inside, which meant someone broke in...*No! I never should've left her alone, now I have to find her!*

Kitty woke up in a small warehouse, tied to a chair.

"Oh! Hello, I've been waiting for you to wake up." A British voice told her.

"Gordon?! You're working with Larry?! Oh." Kitty turned her head around to see that Gordon was also tied to a chair. Gordon smiled at her.

"I'm terribly sorry about what happened at the gas station...The Master told me that *you* were the one that's evil and needed to be stopped. But once Larry tied me to this chair and said he was going to shove me into a portal for experimentation, I realized that *he* was evil and needed to be stopped."

"Okay- but, you don't just explode a person and- WAIT, DID YOU SAY HE WAS GOING TO SHOVE YOU INTO A PORTAL?!"

"Yes, I am afraid I did."

"We have to get out of here. And I never thought I'd say this, but I might need you to help me, but this *doesn't* mean I forgive you, and once we're out I'm going to throw you right back in jail. For now, though...We need to escape."

"Well, I don't mean to be rude, but can't your friends help us?"

"Daniel left and Dog and I had an argument."

"Oh...That's very unfortunate. I'm very sorry."

"Anyways, I have a plan." Kitty hesitated, realizing she actually doesn't have a plan.

"Maybe you can get me out so I can assist you?" Gordon suggested.

"Yeah right, so you can get out and leave *me* here." Then she remembered all the training exercises that she did with Dog. For some reason, there was one that was exactly like this; a two person scenario where both of the people had gotten captured. So she decided to get Gordon out of the ropes. It was a bit of a strange process... she had to try to move her chair to be back-to-back with Gordon's so she could use her hands- which were sticking out the back of the chair- to untie his ropes. It was hard because she couldn't she what she was doing, and it took a bit longer than she would've liked, but Kitty eventually succeeded and Gordon was freed from the chair.

"Ah! Thank you very much. Now I can help you." Gordon smiled. Kitty was lost on ideas, so she just decided to follow the rest of the scenario. The first step was to locate the nearest air vent. Kitty saw one, and after Gordon untied her, she walked up to it.

"Gordon, I need you to help me up there." The vent was about ten feet up, and both of them together were about that high. Gordon stood next to her and helped her up to the vent. She stood on his shoulders and broke the vent open.

"Hey! It's going to cost at *least* ten dollars to replace that." Gordon frowned.

"Our lives or Larry's money?" She climbed into the vent, which was thankfully one of those big air vents that you see in spy movies. She helped Gordon up and they both started to crawl forward.

"So...How do we know when we can get out?" Gordon asked.

"Well, we can just look through the grate." They kept crawling until they reached one, and Kitty looked through it. It looked like it led outside, so Kitty kicked it open. Gordon dropped down first, and then caught Kitty. It was a nice gesture, but Kitty still glared at him. "Now, we have to get you back in prison."

Gordon frowned.

"You committed arson and attempted murder. That's illegal." Kitty told him.

"I understand..." Gordon sighed, giving her a sad look. "But, it's just...I was in prison...And then I got kidnapped..." Gordon stared at her with big, sad eyes.

"You were in prison for a reason-" Kitty sighed. "Fine. I'll give you *one day*. But then I'm turning you in again." Gordon smiled. And then the Master appeared out of nowhere.

"Agent Kitty. It seems you have survived. Not surprising, since that sword was only meant to... ah, put you into a state of paralysis. But I'm afraid I must kidnap you again."

"How can you *always* find me, but you never find Dog?!"

"Well, I don't just need Agent Dog I need you too. And you're annoying." The Master lunged forward at her with his sword, but Gordon jumped in the way. The Master stopped and just stared at him. "Gordon, what- what are you doing?" The Master paused, but then just shoved Gordon out of the way and sprinted towards Kitty. She side-stepped out of the way and kicked the back of his knee, but... there wasn't anything solid except for the cloak he was wearing. It was like kicking air.

The Master took advantage of her surprise and smacked her head with the flat side of his sword, knocking her over. Gordon stepped forward, but stopped when the Master put his blade near Kitty's neck. Gordon hesitated.

"*Don't* get Dog!" Kitty cried out to Gordon.

"Oh! Great idea. Go get Dog. We'll be here..." The Master gave Gordon a map, then snapped his fingers and he and Kitty disappeared.

Of course, the first thing Gordon did was go get Dog. He politely asked around, wanting to know if anybody had seen him. Many people said he'd been looking around at several suspicious locations. Gordon followed someone's directions to an abandoned house and found Dog there, sitting on the ground.

"Oh! Hello there! I've been looking all over the city for you." Gordon called to him. Dog stared at Gordon, looking furious.

"*YOU*! Kidnapping Kitty once wasn't enough?!" He stood up, his fur bristling aggressively.

"Pardon me? I didn't kidnap her. Larry did. She helped me escape, and then someone else came and kidnapped her again. She told me *not* to get you...But I can't rescue her on my own."

Dog growled at him. "You expect me to believe that?"

"Well...Yes, I do. If you don't, then who's going to save her?" Gordon explained, looking innocently at Dog.

"Why do *you* want to save her?"

"I feel bad for trying to kill her and I want to make it up to her."

"Fine. Where is she?"

"The one who kidnapped her gave me a map; he said that he wanted you to find him." Gordon handed it to Dog. The laundromat was circled. They both got into a car someone had given to Dog and drove there.

While that was happening...

The Master tied Kitty to a chair. She'd really had enough of chairs at this point.

"And now, we just have to wait for Dog." The Master looked towards the door. Kitty had no idea where it led, or where she was. She knew that she was in some sort of underground base, because there were no windows... and there was a sign on the wall that said "Underground Base". Kitty looked around the room and saw that it was a fairly small square; no bigger than about thirty feet in each direction. The walls and floor were gray, seemingly made from concrete, and in one corner of the room were a few desks with computers. Directly in front of Kitty and to her right were both doors, and the only exits. On the wall between them was a rack full of various weapons.

"Well you'll be waiting a long time. He's not going to come for me." Kitty told the Master confidently, looking back at him. She wasn't lying to him; she did believe that Gordon wouldn't bring Dog. And she was barely afraid of what the Master would do to her. After all, she'd already died once.

"And what makes you say that?" The Master turned to Kitty quizzically.

"Gordon isn't going to get him. He's just a psychopath that locked me in a gas station and tried to blow me up."

The Master paused at that[7]. "Well. In that case, you're not of much use, are you?" The Master then clapped his hands. "Samuel! Where are you?"

A man came into the room that looked *just* like Daniel, though he had a scarf around his face so Kitty couldn't tell. "Hello, Master!" He sounded like Daniel too. So Kitty just had to ask:

"Daniel? Is that you?"

Samuel turned to Kitty in surprise and seemed like he wanted to say something, but stopped himself. Instead he told her, "Daniel? Who's Daniel? I'm... uh, I'm Samuel! I've never heard of anyone named Samu- I mean, Daniel." He responded.

"Samuel. This is Agent Kitty. She isn't of any use any more. And you need to prove your loyalty. *You know what to do.*"

"Uh, yes. Of course." Samuel took a weapon off the wall and grabbed Kitty. She didn't resist because despite 'Samuel's' protests, he probably was Daniel. He led her towards the door that had been in front of her, but the Master followed.

"Um... uh, Master, sir..."

"Yes?" The Master replied.

"I'd feel more comfortable if I did this alone... I'm- uh, self-conscious about this kind stuff..."

"You're self-conscious about killing someone?" The Master asked bluntly.

Daniel- or, Samuel- nodded slowly.

"Oh well. Who am I to judge? Go on ahead." The Master patted Samuel on the shoulder, and whispered to him: "...I know a good therapist for this kind of stuff." The Master handed a piece of folded paper to Samuel, who nodded and put it in his pocket.

Samuel then continued through the door and pushed Kitty up a ladder, which led to a very small room.

Samuel took off his scarf, which confirmed Kitty's thoughts about him being Daniel.

"Daniel! I knew it was you. What are you doing here?!" Kitty asked him.

"Shh! Quiet! I decided that I could be of more use as a secret spy. So I came up with a secret identity! A very convincing one, I might add. And the Master was desperate enough for more employees that he hired me on the spot!" Daniel opened a door that led outside, and shoved Kitty through. "Now, get out! There aren't any guards right now, so you need to go!"

"But- what about you? What if he finds out? You have to come with me!"

"No way! I can be of way more use here."

"Okay...Just don't do anything you might regret." Kitty paused, and then ran out. The ocean was right there, which would've been pretty if Kitty wasn't hydrophobic. So she just ran as far as she could and then realized she was completely and totally lost.

Chapter eight

Gordon and Dog pulled up at the laundromat in two bikes that they had rented. There were arrows on the floor pointing to an open trapdoor. They both went in, having to crawl down a ladder, and they walked down an *insanely* long hallway. They eventually arrived at a door, and went in. Inside was a fairly small room, and there stood a man with a black hood and a Japanese fox mask. Next to him was a guy that looked just like Daniel, but he had a scarf over his face so Dog couldn't tell.

"Agent Dog?!" The Master exclaimed, surprise in his voice. "Well, this didn't go the way I was expecting."

"Where's Kitty?!" He growled.

"Oh...Well, I didn't think you were coming, or else I would've kept her alive."

Gordon gasped behind Dog. "You didn't! You're *very, VERY* rude."

"WHAT. DID. YOU. DO?!" Dog growled, taking a threatening step forward.

"Oh, she's dead." The Master simply shrugged.

"No! You're lying!" Dog cried out. The other guy ran towards Dog and winked at him. He shoved Dog and Gordon back and closed the door before they could react, then took off his scarf. "DANIEL! YOU *LET* HIM KILL KITTY?! I HAD TRUSTED YOU!" Dog snarled.

"What? No! I went undercover to find out some of their secrets, and then he brought Kitty here, and told me to... you know-"

"*You* killed Kitty?!" Gordon gasped.

"No! Don't interrupt me! Of *course* I would never. So I let her go. I just didn't think you were coming, so now we have to find her before she gets kidnapped again."

Dog knew he was joking about the last part, but the scary thing was that it was actually a possibility. Lots of people would want to have Kitty, either for revenge against Dog or bargaining.

"Let's go find her! She can't have gone very far." Gordon said cheerfully.

"Yeah! WAIT A MINUTE. GORDON?!" Daniel stared at Gordon.

"What? I'd like to help you find Kitty. Is that so weird?"

"Well, yeah! You locked her in a gas station that you then exploded."

"I'd appreciate it if everyone stopped pointing that out." Gordon frowned.

The Master's giant sword smashed through the door, barely missing Daniel. "Ah! We should *probably* get out of here." He said, running down the hall with Gordon and Dog following. They raced out of the secret entrance into the laundromat.

"Daniel, what direction did Kitty go?" Dog asked.

"Well the thing is, we went out the *other* entrance. So from here? I have no idea."

"So, how are we going to go back into the tunnel, fight the Master, break back into the secret base- which probably has guards all over now- and then go through the *other* tunnel and *then* try to remember what direction Kitty went, and *THEN* try to run fast enough to catch up to her, assuming she hasn't changed directions?" Dog frowned, looking back into the tunnel.

"Oh, don't worry. I can handle the Master." Gordon jumped down the secret entrance.

"Um, okay then." Dog watched as Gordon ran off.

"All right, it's safe!" Gordon yelled. Dog and Daniel jumped down and saw the Master and Gordon drinking some tea.

"What the-" Daniel stared at the Master

"Anyone can appreciate some good tea." Gordon smiled. The Master reached into his pocket and grabbed out a pen and a piece of paper.

"What *is* this tea? I have to write it down. HAHA! JUST KIDDING!" The Master clicked the pen four times and his giant sword erupted from it.

"Woah! That's cool!" Daniel shouted, taking off his hat. "EVERYONE! BACK AWAY!" He threw it at the Master, and the hat exploded. The entire tunnel caved in, nearly smashing everyone. "Whoops!"

The Master stepped out of the rubble, but a crack was on his mask. He growled, his sword glowing brighter.

Suddenly, Gordon screamed. "NO! MY TEA CUPS! THOSE WERE MY GREAT-GREAT-GREAT GRANDMA'S!" Gordon fell to the ground, sobbing.

"Seriously?" Daniel sighed.

"*You will pay for this.*" Gordon slowly got up, glaring furiously at the Master. Gordon moved with surprising speed as he raced towards the Master and punched him in the face... or, well, his mask. The Master stumbled backwards and Gordon ripped his mask off. There wasn't a face behind it though... there wasn't *anything*. Black smoke poured out, and he appeared to deflate, the clothes falling onto the floor. The black smoke rose up, morphing into a human shape again and holding the sword.

"Oh, you don't know what you've just done." His clothes floated off the floor too, and onto his smoky body. The mask repaired itself, hovering onto his face- well if he had one.

"Okay- you have to admit, that's kind of cool!" Daniel smiled, looking up at the strange figure. The Master started floating back to the ground, and used all of the debris to create a huge throne for himself. Larry came out behind him, from the door that led to the hideout, frowning.

"That cave-in wasn't funny, the Master- that name is weird, I had *such* a hard time opening the door. Anyways, are you ready to open that portal to another dimension?"

"*Larry!*" Dog snarled.

"You need to apologize for locking us in that bunker! *It had no internet!*" Daniel glared at Larry.

"*No internet*?! You really *are* rude!" Gordon gasped.

SECRETS OF THE AGENCY

"Bye!" The Master said, grabbing Larry and bursting out of the roof.

Chapter nine

Kitty frowned, and turned around to where she thought she came from. But it didn't look familiar. She ran in that direction anyway. Who'd have thought being lost would be so confusing? *Okay, okay, let's focus here...* She stared at a tree, taking in its appearance. Kitty then continued walking, before realizing that there was absolutely no point in memorizing that tree.

The Master and Larry suddenly appeared in front of her, though luckily their backs turned to her. They were facing a large clearing, and Kitty crouched down behind a tree, hoping that they didn't turn around. The Master snapped and a large, metal circle popped into existence in front of them. Along with a shoe.

"Oh! I wondered where that was." Larry picked it up. "I just wonder where my other one went... Anyways, how long will it take to open up that portal?"

"Well, we have to find a sufficient power source. AKA kidnapping someone because it's powered by human energy." The Master said, walking towards the metal circle, which Kitty now noticed had wires all over it that connecting to some sort of metal contraption.

"We just had two humans back there! Why didn't we take one?"

The Master paused. "*Darn it.*" He whispered to himself. "That's why I have *you*, Larry. You think of these things!" The Master disappeared and came back with Gordon, Daniel, and Dog. He threw Daniel down, placing the contraption on his head while Larry tied Gordon and Dog up with chain. Dog stared at Larry with hatred in his eyes. Kitty suspected that Larry had made a threat so that Dog wouldn't resist.

"Oooh! This feels weird." Daniel laughed.

Kitty resisted the urge to leap out with her axe right then. *This is all on me...* She realized. With the others tied up, she was the only one left to stop them from opening the portal. Well- that probably wasn't true, but she was the only one in close proximity. She reached for her axe, getting ready to jump, but when she did, the Master turned around and clicked his pen, blocking her way with the sword.

"Don't think I forgot about you." The Master chuckled, bringing his sword up close to her.

"Kitty, don't! Get away!" Dog cried out to her, but she ignored him.

Larry turned on the portal and a big red light formed in the center of the circle, slowly getting bigger until it filled up the entire circle[8]. Only a few seconds passed before a strange figure came out. It looked like one of Dog's kind! Dog stared at the figure in surprise. The Master stepped up close to the person.

"Y-you!" The person had a look of fear on his face and took a step back. "What do you want?!"

"I want *answers*, Jeremy."

Kitty glanced at the control panel. She had an idea...but it was probably horrible. Jeremy looked around, squinting from the brightness. He looked down. "You should've thought of that before trying to kill me."

The Master swung his sword at Jeremy, who ducked down right in time. The Master practically growled in rage. "You brought it upon yourself! YOU DID THIS TO ME!" The Master showed his arm, which was completely made of black smoke.

Jeremy's eyes widened. "I... I didn't know. It was an experiment... you agreed to it! You knew the risks!"

Kitty glanced at Daniel. Powering the machine was definitely taking a toll on him. That's when she made her decision. Kitty jumped forward, pushing the Master into the portal. He dropped his sword in surprise. The momentum pulled Kitty through the portal too, as she had expected would happen. At the last moment, she threw her axe at the control panel and the portal closed behind her.

"WHAT HAVE YOU DONE?!" The Master yelled, looking around this area. It was completely red, and Kitty wasn't able to tell where it ended.

She looked away. "I did what I had to do."

"You realize that you're completely defenseless? You threw away your axe. I could kill you easily.

"Well, at least you won't be able to hurt anyone else."

"You think you're so brave, sacrificing yourself for your friends? Well guess what. That man I brought out of the portal is the ex-leader of the Suspicious People. And without me to stop him, he'll destroy the world. So you just doomed *everyone*."

"Wait- if he's a different species, would he really be a 'man' as in hu-man? What's that species even called, and shouldn't you address him as his proper species name thing?"

"*Seriously? That's* what you're worried about?"

"What? I don't want to be impolite." Kitty then blushed, realizing how much she sounded like Gordon. Then she blushed harder because she realized she was blushing.

"NO!" Dog yelled. Daniel had fainted from the portal taking his energy, but Dog honestly didn't care. Kitty had just been *sucked up by a giant portal to another dimension*! And there was no way to get her out. Why did she have to be like this? Why does she always feel the need to sacrifice herself? Dog had it under control, but Kitty just *had* to take things into her own hands! And now look what happened to her!

"This is quite unfortunate." Gordon frowned.

In Daniel's mind...

Huh? Hello! Anyone alive...? Oh this is my mind. Daniel gasped- in his mind. *Sqauntalius Dingle Head the third! My first imaginary friend. How have you been?* Sqauntalius Dingle Head the third slowly faded away. *W-what?* The feeling of the empty white void and his echoey voice soon got to him. *Am... I still alive?*

A few memories popped up... him making his first friend (Squantalius Dingle Head the third)...him with Kitty...*Kitty!* Daniel heard Dog shouting her name, and wasn't sure whether it was real or not. Something about a portal...

"Kitty! KITTY! Why did you JUMP INTO A PORTAL?!" Dog shouted at the metal circle. Jeremy put his hand on Dog's shoulder.

"There's nothing we can do." Jeremy was the one who had broken Dog out of his ropes. Since their species numbers were so small, they had to do what they can to stick together. Larry laid unconscious off to the side while Jeremy untied Gordon.

Daniel felt (or didn't feel?) imaginary tears on his face. *It was nice living...* Suddenly a rush of cold came over him...But it was wet. And icy. He jumped awake, all wet with Dog holding an empty bucket over him. Icy water was pooled around Daniel's feet.

"DOG! WHAT THE HECK!?" Daniel shouted in anger

Dog had a sad look on his face.

"What? What's wrong?" Daniel asked with a soft voice. If Dog was showing visible emotion, something must be very wrong.

"Kitty jumped into a portal to an alternate dimension, and now she's trapped in there with the Master."

"Oh, cool... WHAT!?" Daniel's voice was calm for about five seconds before realizing what Dog had actually said. "How do we open the portal again to save her?"

Dog and Jeremy looked at each other sadly. "We...we can't. She smashed the control panel."

"Oh. I know one way we could possibly save her..." Daniel told them both. Daniel was glad he knew of this technique to save her, otherwise he would have been absolutely freaking out. "So, what we do is we get this really crispy chicken nugget, then we make a circle around it, saying: 'I like waffle fries', and it opens!" He said confidently.

Back in the alternate dimension...

Kitty sat down, bored. She looked at the black void around her. The Master sat down in front of her, looking equally bored. Well, she assumed he was bored, but she couldn't *actually* tell since she couldn't see his face. Kitty got a pencil and notepad out of her pocket. She was glad that she had decided to put them in there. After all, you never know when you might need some!

"Ever play dot monsters?" She asked the Master, unable to hide her grin.

"*What?*"

"Oh! It's a game where you randomly put a bunch of dots on a piece of paper, then connect them to look like an animal." She handed him the pencil and some paper. He stared at her like she was crazy. "What? We're both bored." The Master tore up the paper and broke the pencil. Kitty glared at him. "Well you don't have to ruin *my* fun too."

The portal suddenly re-opened, revealing Dog, Gordon, Daniel, and Jeremy standing in a circle around a pretty crispy chicken nugget.

"IT ACTUALLY WORKED?!" Dog shouted.

Daniel laughed. "Never doubt the chicken nugget."

The Master instantly leapt up, grabbing Kitty and exiting the weird dimension. "Just because you opened the portal, don't think Kitty is safe." He ran off with her.

"Not so fast!" Jeremy shouted. "I still have your pen!" Jeremy clicked the pen six times.

"What's that supposed to do- AH!" The Master's weird smoky body started floating towards the pen. "Stop! STOP!" He screamed as the pen sucked him in. They didn't hear any more from him.

"I think this is officially the weirdest day of my life." Kitty commented, staring at the pen. "Anyways, I guess the Master is taken care of now."

"Yes, he is." Jeremy dug a hole in the ground and dropped the pen in, covering it up.

"What do we do about Larry?" Dog asked. "We can't arrest him since we don't have any evidence against him."

Daniel ate the chicken nugget. "About that...I was secretly recording all the evil stuff he did with a tiny camera I put on him. *Don't ask how.* And I just uploaded the footage to TotallyActualVideos.com and the Agency fired him and re-hired you."

Dog stared at Daniel in amazement. "Wow. I really need to bring you on more missions- WAIT, NO. I DIDN'T MEAN THAT."

"Dog, Daniel just opened an interdimensional portal with a *CHICKEN NUGGET.*" Kitty smiled at Daniel as a way of thanking him.

"What about me?" Gordon asked with hope in his voice. "May I come on a mission or two? Or three? Or five hundred fifty-seven?"

"Sure!" Kitty said quickly, and then realized that she just invited the guy that *tried to kill her* to join her on missions. But...for some reason, she couldn't bring herself to say no.

"Really?" Gordon smiled.

"*Really?*" Dog frowned.

"Yes."

Random interlude
A month later

The Master was stuck in his pen. His plan had not been successful. All thanks to that *Agent Kitty.* She just *had* to be heroic and save everyone. Well, why couldn't someone save the Master for once? Why was he all alone? *It's because you're different...it's because you're made of smoke.* A voice in his mind told him. Though he knew the real reason, his mind refused to believe it. It's why he wanted *revenge.* Revenge against Jeremy for making him like this. Revenge against Kitty for stopping his plans. Revenge against Larry for- well, no reason. He's just Larry.

The Master's rage built up, like a volcano ready to explode. And it did. He felt the pen crack. He leaked out of it, like water. His smoky form passed through the loose dirt. He was uncontainable. Unstoppable. *Unreasonable...* A small voice spoke up...*Irrational...A bad guy...STOP! STOP IT! I'm not bad for wanting revenge against those who wronged me...Yes, yes you are...* He silenced the voice in his head. He needed to focus on one thing and one thing only. *Stopping Agent Kitty. Whatever it took.*

Chapter ten

Kitty sat inside Dog's military base house. It felt nice to be back here; this is where she spent most of her life. Even though Larry had taken everything out, it still felt like home. But Gordon seemed less happy to be here.

"I don't mean to be rude, but this house lacks personality. Not nearly enough tea cups!" He said, frowning. "My great aunt Mary was an interior designer. She always said: *'A house is not a house without an excessive amount of teacups!'*."

Kitty laughed. "I don't think Dog would be mad if we got a few..." It had only been a month, but she's gotten to know Gordon a lot better. He wasn't an insane arsonist, but a nice, polite guy who just hadn't realized that he was being lied to.

Just then, a small crack in the ground started leaking black smoke... but from what?

"Hm? What's that?" Gordon pointed to the ground.

"It looks like...Oh *no*! DOG!" Kitty shouted. Both Dog and Daniel raced over.

"Ew! What's that?" Daniel asked.

"It can't be!" Dog frowned.

The Master took shape in front of them.

"Hello again!" He laughed. "Don't mind me, I'll just be borrowing Dog's body."

"WAIT- WHAT?!" Kitty yelled, quickly grabbing her axe and throwing it at the Master. He swiftly dodged, then slowly moved towards Dog, but Kitty leapt in front of him. "If you want him, you'll have to get me first!"

"And to get her, you'll have to get *me* first!" Gordon said, jumping in front of Kitty.

"Gordon, what-"

The Master just pushed them aside harshly, going in front of Dog. The Master lunged at Dog, but he leapt to the side. "Kitty!" He called out to her. She knew what he wanted. Kitty grabbed her axe from where it had been stuck in the wall and threw it next to Dog, who quickly grabbed in and aimed to cut the Master's mask in half. But the Master's smoke formed into tendrils and went straight up Dog's nose.

"Dog!" Kitty shouted as the Master's mask and cloak appeared on him. The mask fit kind of weird due to Dog's nose, so it didn't look quite right.

"Ah, much better. It's nice to have something that would be actually considered a body, instead of just smoke." The Master- or Dog- or something- said. "Call me... Master Dog." He grinned menacingly.

Master Dog disappeared.

"What. The. Heck. Just. Happened?!" Daniel frowned in confusion. "I think we're going to need more chicken nuggets for this. *Extra crispy.*"

Daniel ran to the grocery store, while Kitty and Gordon tried to plan out their next move. Kitty decided to turn on the news, to see if there were any clues. Surely, the Master planned to do something with Dog's body. And Kitty couldn't really come up with anything else.

"BREAKING NEWS!" The TV said. "The boss of the Agency has turned *evil*. The only information our reporters have been able to gather, is that something called the Agency exists, and the leader of it is a... dog? Anyways, he's now wearing a weird black mask and breaking into power plants across the city! He seems to be teleporting around."

Kitty frowned, looking at the live feed of Master Dog appearing in different places. "C'mon. We need to get to the Brookstone Village power plant."

"You mean...a mission? Just us?" Gordon asked, smiling widely.

"Yeah! Now, let's go!" Kitty left a quick note for Daniel then drove off with Gordon to go find Dog.

They arrived at the power plant, and Kitty saw Dog driving away. "FOLLOW HIM!" She yelled. Then realized she was the one driving.

She quickly chased after him, probably going over the speed limit. He was obviously trying to lose her. She stayed on his tail, and eventually they reached a- NUCLEAR REACTOR?! She didn't even realize that there was one in Brookstone Village! Master Dog raced inside with a pretty large power generator in his hands. Kitty and Gordon snuck quietly in after him. They passed through a lot of hallways. They went into the reactor room[9], assuming that's where Master Dog would be since Kitty lost sight of him. They entered, and there he was. The reactor room was like a big computer room; there were levers, buttons, and cords everywhere. And through a glass wall was a giant, blinding sphere.

"Ah, I've been waiting for you..." Master Dog turned towards Kitty.

"Give me back Dog." She took a threatening step forward.

"Or what? You'll weakly attack me, I'll capture you, and then wait for someone else to come and finish me off?"

Kitty frowned. "I don't just get kidnapped. I can finish you off myself." She held her axe in a defensive position.

"Sure you can." Master Dog snapped his fingers and Daniel and Gordon appeared behind him, both tied up. "Mm... with all this energy around, my powers are increasing." He turned around, facing Daniel and Gordon, who both just looked completely confused. Kitty took her chance and jumped at him, realizing too late that it was a trap. Master Dog turned around again, pulling out his gigantic sword. He effortlessly brought his sword up, using it as a shield against Kitty's attack. His sword made a crackling sound as Kitty got launched back from the power of his it. She hit the wall, falling on the ground. Master Dog stepped towards her, dragging his sword on the ground, which made a horrible screeching sound. "Face it, Kitty. You're just a sidekick, and that's all you'll ever be."

Kitty got up and ran towards Master Dog, dodging under his sword. She almost hit him with her axe before remembering that it was Dog. She froze. *I can't hurt him...* she thought.

"Now, put down the axe; you don't really need it. You're just a sidekick, after all."

"You're overusing that word!" She yelled, knocking him over. Her actions had caught him by surprise, leaving her a two second window of opportunity. She smacked him on the nose, not hard enough to hurt him, but enough to...It was really weird, but hopefully he'd sneeze the Master out...Dogs sneezed if you hit them on the nose, right[10]? Apparently so, because it worked! As he sneezed, the black smoke came pouring out of his nose. Dog collapsed, but Kitty caught him. "Dog...Come on, wake up."

"Why? So he can save you?" The Master laughed, rising up. Weird white things were going into him. Uh oh. Was he *absorbing* the nuclear energy? The Master was really weird. He got twice as big, no, three times as big. Kitty really hoped that none of them got radiation poisoning from this. She laid Dog by the wall, where he'd hopefully be safe from the Master's attacks. The Master's sword was about to hit Kitty when it was stopped by... Gordon? With a vacuum cleaner? It must have been a pretty dull sword...

"Now, let's handle this like gentlemen." He said. "You stay next to Dog, in case he wakes up during... this." Gordon told Kitty, holding up the handheld vacuum cleaner and started to suck up the Master.

"Um, are you sure that will work?"

"Positive! It's an industrial grade vacuum. The box said 'It will suck up anything!' and I don't see why they'd lie."

"Hey, hey stop that!" The Master yelled at Gordon. "HEY!" The Master disappeared inside the vacuum container, mask and all. Except for his sword, which returned to pen form and clattered on the ground.

"Kitty..." Dog said softly.

"Yeah?" She turned to him.

"You just defeated the Master."

"No, it was a team effort. Gordon was the one who actually defeated him, I just helped."

Dog shook his head. "If you hadn't been there, Gordon never would've been able to defeat him."

Kitty smiled. She *had* done something other than get kidnapped for once! Even if it wasn't *really* defeating the Master.

Chapter eleven

Two months later

Kitty and Gordon sat outside Dog's house, in the small side yard. Ever since Gordon sucked the Master up with the vacuum, they'd both been incredibly worried that he'd escape. So Gordon had put the vacuum in an industrial strength plastic bag, and he was confident it would keep anything from escaping. He was so adorably trusting in companies. He abruptly jumped out of his chair.

"Kitty..." He said slowly, his back turned to her as he reached for something in his pocket. "I know this may be sudden, but I've made my decision... and I ask that you make one too." Gordon turned around, dropped onto one knee, and held a silver ring up to Kitty. "Will you marry me?"

The golden light from the setting sun lit up Gordon's face, making this moment seem way more dramatic.

"Sure," Kitty hesitated, not really sure what to do.

Gordon seemed surprised for a second, then relieved, and then he slipped the ring onto her finger.

Daniel ran into the side yard. "Um, what's going on?" He asked, looking confused. Kitty blushed. "Never mind; DOG IS GOING BACK IN THAT WEIRD INTERDIMENSIONAL PORTAL THING AGAIN! He found another chicken nugget that was just the right amount of crispy, and he must've gotten two more people to stand around it in a circle with!"

"Huh?" Kitty and Gordon said in unison.

"No time!" Daniel grabbed both of them and shoved them in his car. Then they all got out, realizing that Dog had a helicopter, which would be faster. Then they got back in, realizing that Dog had taken his helicopter. So they all drove to the airport and flew to Red Mountain City, which was actually quicker in a commercial airplane for some reason. They got a taxi and went to the portal as fast as possible, not questioning how the taxi driver knew where it was, and they got there just in time. The portal was open, and Dog was nearly in.

"DOG! DON'T!" Kitty shouted, running out towards him.

"I have to." He responded solemnly.

"What? No you don't!"

"Who knows what's in here? It could be more of my kind. Jeremy already left, but because of having him here... I realized what I've been missing."

"But...what if you can't find your way back? It's too dangerous!"

"Don't worry. I'll find my way back." And with that, he stepped into the portal. There wasn't really a way to close it, so he just left it open. Kitty watched him walk out of sight, knowing that there wasn't really anything that she could do. Though, she wondered how it was being powered. She looked at the power wires, and they were connected to a...*of course.* A chicken nugget.

Kitty went back to the house, sad that Dog left, but sure that he would come back soon. She found a note on Dog's bed. It was a map...to a science facility? The note said...

"As you know, my species is uncomfortable with the concept of 'birth' so we made a cloning machine to make offspring. Anyways, I decided that I would clone myself, for two reasons:

In case I don't make it back from the portal, and because my species numbers are so small. Here's the map to where the cloning machine is. Make sure to pick my clone up in one month. DON'T FORGET!"

Well. That was weird.

Epilogue

Nine years later

A lot had happened in nine years. Which wasn't surprising, considering nine years was a really long time. Kitty and Gordon had moved into the cabin after picking up Dog's clone (Who was fittingly named Dog Jr, with the nickname DJ) and Kitty also had a daughter...Which she named Addi, after her mom, Addison.

Addi came into the living room from outside, hiding behind her long, blonde hair.

"Addi? What's wrong?" Kitty asked.

"DJ said my dolls look weird!" Addi cried, running forward and hugging Kitty. DJ came in.

"I only did it because she called my action figures dolls!" He said, glaring at Addi.

"Well, they are!" Addi defended herself.

"How'd you like it if I called your dolls action figures?!"

"I'D LIKE IT JUST FINE BECAUSE I DON'T COMPLAIN!" Addi shouted.

"Kids! Kids! I want you *both* to apologize." Kitty frowned, putting her hands on both of their shoulders.

"Sorry..." They said to each other, before running off.

Gordon came in the door, smiling. Since Dog had gone through the portal, Gordon had been the new boss of the Agency. They wanted the kids to have a somewhat normal life though, so they didn't tell them, because the Agency was pretty weird sometimes.

Though Kitty had the feeling that it would be pretty hard to hide it from them now... No other job makes enough money to buy four tickets to outer space. Which is what Gordon had brought home.

Epilogue two

The vacuum cracked. It's been nine years. *I'm ready for revenge.* The vacuum broke open and black smoke poured out, searching for its prey...

What we all contributed:

Kendall Schwinn took care of a lot of the writing and did all the editing, proofreading, and drew the cover. And she wrote the characters of Kitty, Gordon, Larry, and all the side characters. (She also wrote all the footnotes[11].)

Jack Plooy took care of most of the storyline, quite a bit of the writing, and was the inspiration behind this entire book. He also wrote the characters of Dog and the Master.

Benicio Pinto wrote nearly all of Daniel's dialogue and actions. And along with writing a fair amount of the storyline, he also added many random elements of fun. You have him to thank for the chicken nuggets.

Kitty, Dog, Daniel, and Gordon will return in:
Secrets of the Agency Two!

SECRETS OF THE AGENCY

Secret epilogue

Dog wandered around in the portal. It had faded from red to a deep black. He swore sometimes he could see his own reflection. He had lost sight of the portal entrance long ago. He was exhausted, but he didn't want to fall asleep. Who knew what was lurking around in the darkness? *Was* it even dark, or was that just the color of the walls? Were there even walls?! Whenever he started to regret his decision, he reminded himself why he came into the portal. *To find more of my kind.* If Jeremy had been in here, who knew who else would be? He knew it was too much to hope, but...what if Addison was in here? Ever since that night, he had wondered if maybe she hadn't died, maybe something had happened to her, and she was waiting for someone to come and rescue her...

He could almost see her in his reflection, standing next to him. He could almost imagine her saying *It's okay, Cheese.* She smiled. *I forgive you. Thank you for taking care of my daughter.* Maybe he was getting too tired, or maybe he could actually hear her voice. Either way, he finally laid down and went to sleep.

Thanks for reading! I hope you enjoyed this book that all three of us worked very hard on.

Book two will be out soon, and we're also planning a prequel!

See you in the next book!

---

[1] "Slightly" secret, as in it's *supposed* to be a secret, but you won't get arrested or anything if you tell someone.

[2] Exactly what it sounds like; a virus that only affects Dog's species. It's what nearly wiped all of them out.

[3] The Suspicious People are an infamous terrorist group. They haven't necessarily done anything bad (at least, within many years) but everyone knows they're evil.

[4] Which he was able to do through an app on his phone, which constantly tracks his coordinates and gives them to the shipping company.

[5] The whole time he was gone, he still had his phone and everyone's numbers, he just never answered anyone's calls

[6] Long story. Don't worry, we're planning to make a prequel to explain this.

[7] The Master doesn't know Gordon that well, so when he saw him with Kitty, he had assumed that Gordon betrayed him, and therefore thought that he would go get Dog.

[8] About ten feet in diameter

[9] There were signs pointing the way to it.

[10] Cats do, at least... I FOUND THIS OUT BY ACCIDENT, I LOVE MY CAT, I SWEAR! -Kendall

[11] Hi ☺